For Saffron and Barnaby
– *G.A.*

This book is dedicated to Tony for his constant
support and good humor
– *D.W.*

Publisher's note: Many thanks to the Natural History Museum of London for their help with this book.

tiger tales would like to thank Anthony Paino of the Academy of Natural Science in Philadelphia.

Pteranodon and Ichthyosaurus lived in the dinosaur era, but they are not technically dinosaurs.

Other books by Giles Andreae and David Wojtowycz:

Commotion in the Ocean   Cock-a-doodle-doo! Barnyard Hullabaloo   Rumble in the Jungle

tiger tales

an imprint of ME Media, LLC

202 Old Ridgefield Road, Wilton, CT 06897

First published in the Untied States 2005 by **tiger tales**

Originally published in Great Britain by Orchard Books, London

Text © 2004 Giles Andreae; Illustrations © 2004 David Wojtowycz

CIP data available

ISBN 1-58925-044-3

Dinosaurs Galore!

by

Giles Andreae

Illustrated by

David Wojtowycz

As the sun lights the horizon,
and the mist begins to clear,
what shapes do you begin to see;
what noises do you hear?

Perhaps you'll see a swishing tail,
huge footprints, or a beak.
I think I heard a distant roar . . .
and did you hear that shriek?

Some of them have huge long necks,
and some have giant jaws.
So let's go to the swampland,
and meet the dinosaurs!

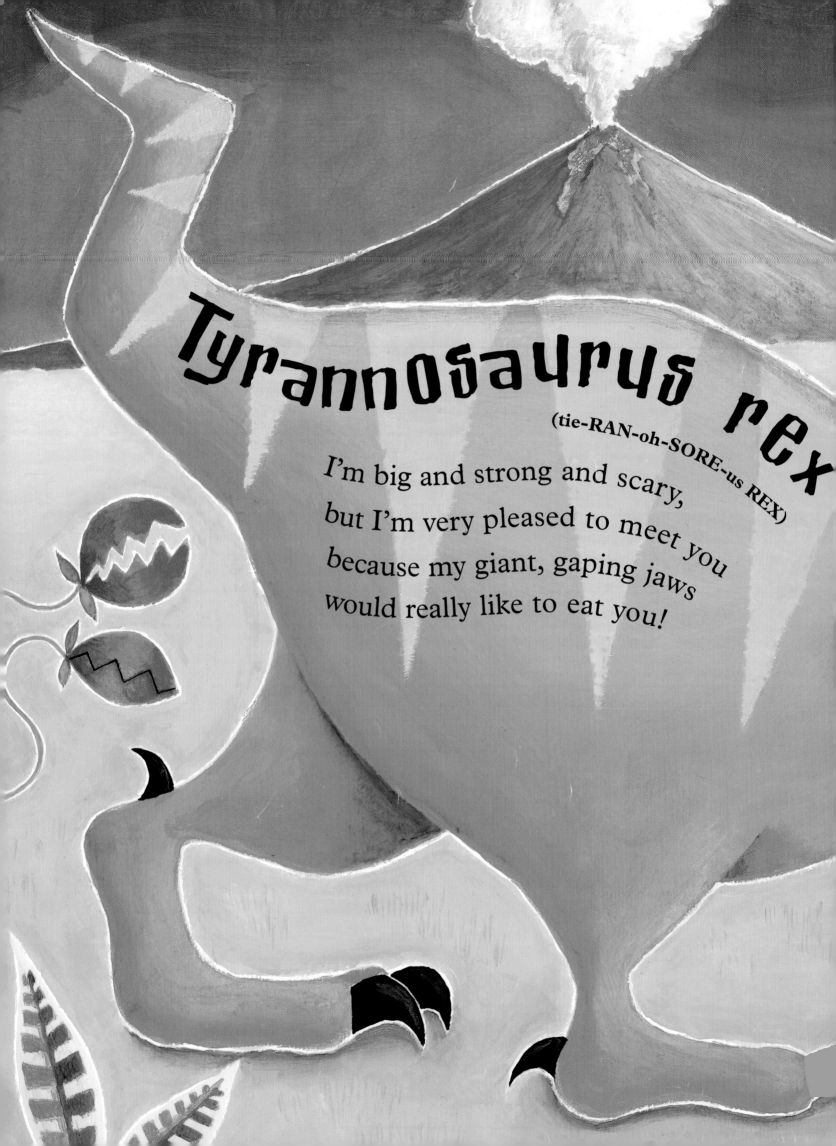

Tyrannosaurus rex

(tie-RAN-oh-SORE-us REX)

I'm big and strong and scary,
but I'm very pleased to meet you
because my giant, gaping jaws
would really like to eat you!

Ankylosaurus
(an-KEE-loh-SORE-us)

I've got armor on the top of me,
and tough skin underneath.
So if you try to eat me up,
you'll really hurt your teeth!

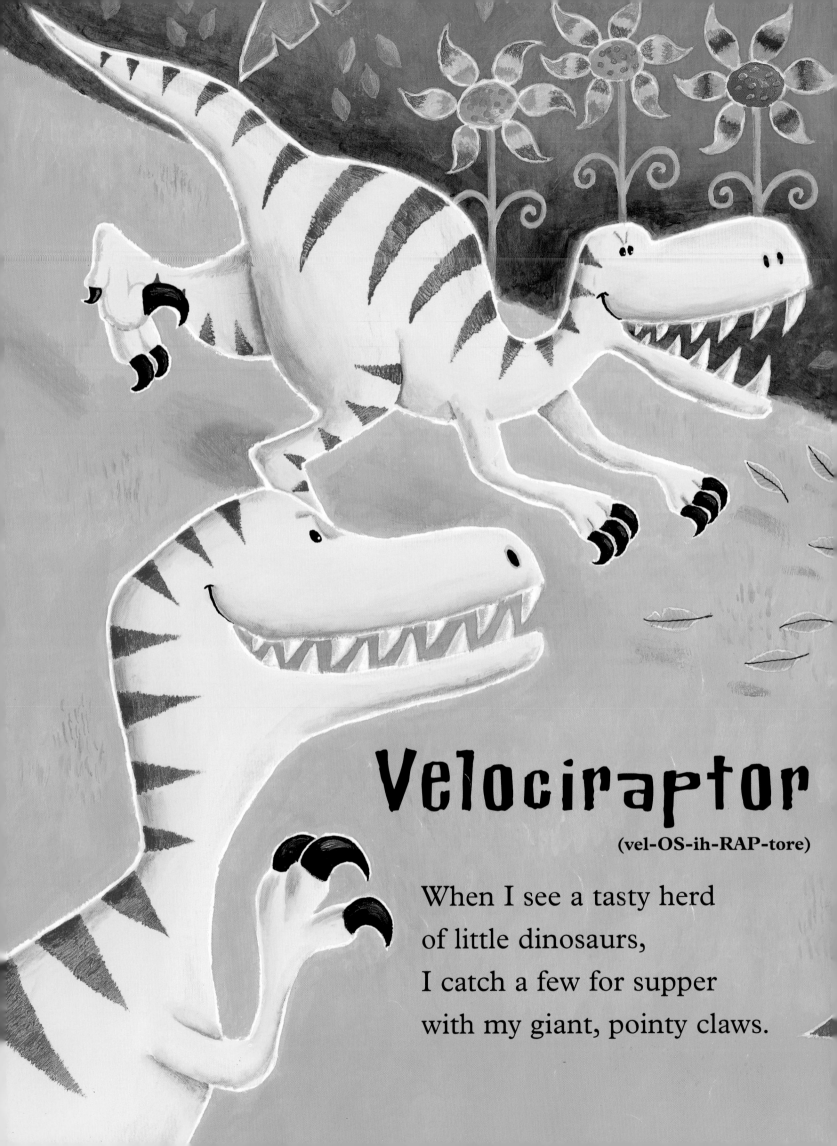

Velociraptor
(vel-OS-ih-RAP-tore)

When I see a tasty herd
of little dinosaurs,
I catch a few for supper
with my giant, pointy claws.

Microraptor

(MY-cro-RAP-tor)

I'm as little as a chicken,
but please don't be too hasty!
Although I may be chicken-sized,
I'm nowhere near as tasty!

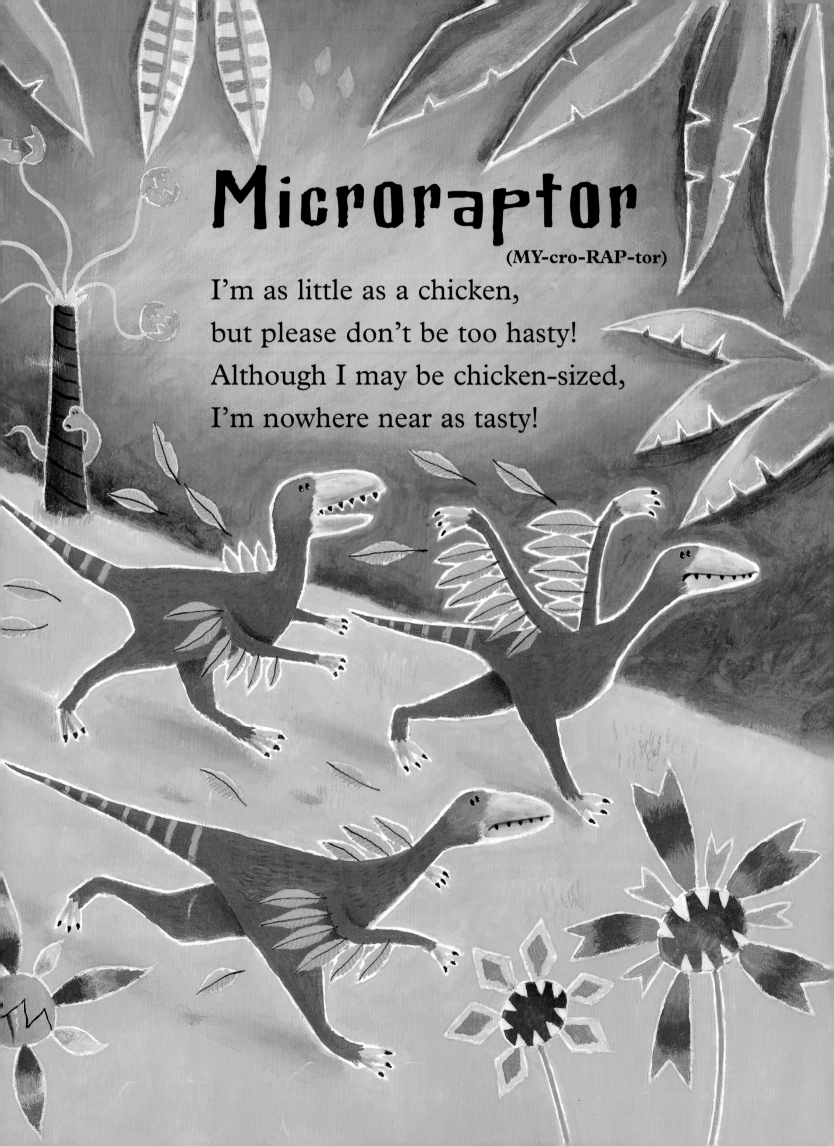

Diplodocus

(die-PLOH-dah-kus)

I'm not the quickest thinker
'cause my brain is very small.
But who needs to be clever
when you're thirty-five feet tall?

Spinosaurus

(SPIE-noh-SORE-us)

I'm sure you can see the big sail on my back;
I use it for storing up heat.
It's also quite handy for making new friends
'cause everyone says it looks neat!

Triceratops

(trie-SAIR-ah-TOPS)

I'm the Triceratops, how do you do?
I've got these three horns on my head.
They're useful for keeping my enemies back,
but they're not very comfy in bed!

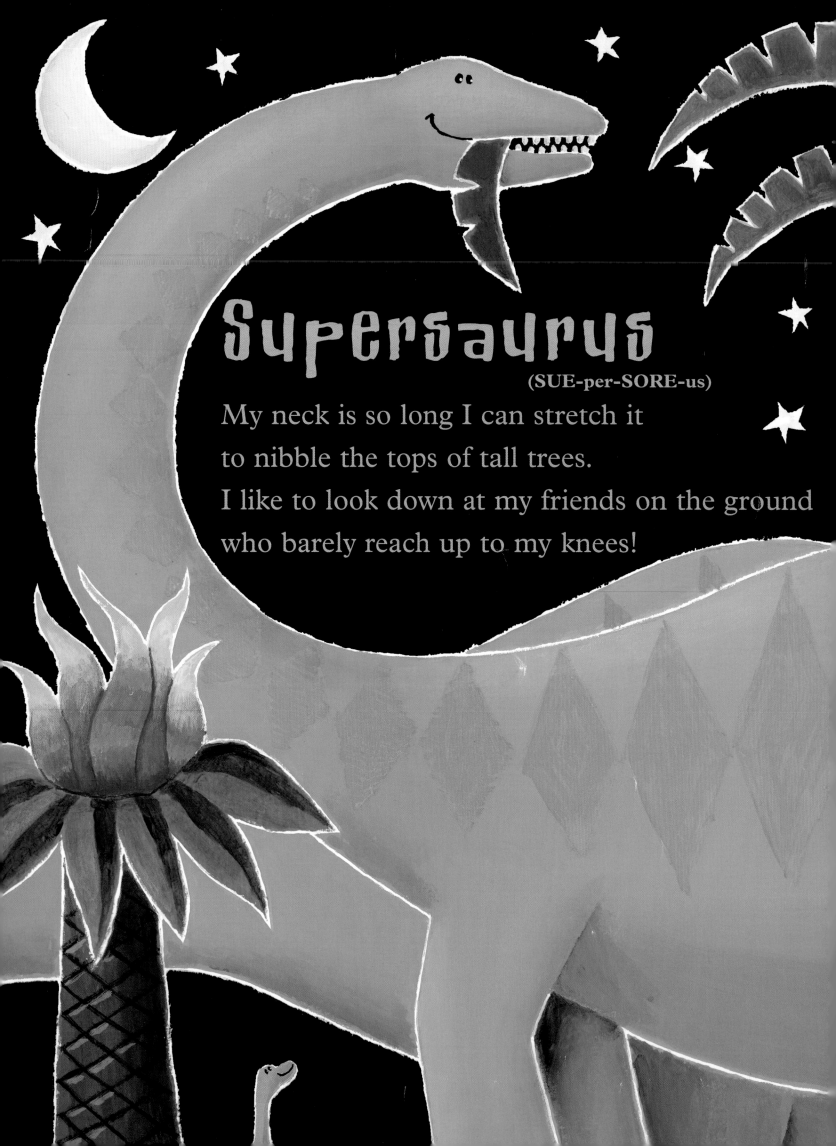

Supersaurus
(SUE-per-SORE-us)

My neck is so long I can stretch it
to nibble the tops of tall trees.
I like to look down at my friends on the ground
who barely reach up to my knees!

Pteranodon
(ter-AN-oh-don)

See the crest upon my head?
It helps me when I glide.
And the girls say it looks groovy
as I swoop from side to side!

Ichthyosaurus

(IK-thee-oh-SORE-us)

I'm a swimming reptile,
I dive down in the sea.
And when I spot a yummy squid,
I eat it up with glee!

Stegosaurus
(STEG-oh-SORE-us)

I am the stout Stegosaurus,
with two rows of plates down my back.
I've also got spikes on the end of my tail,
which I use when I'm under attack!

Giganotosaurus

(JEE-ga-NO-toe-SORE-us)

I am enormous and fierce and strong.
I live by the shores of the lake.
There's a rumbling sound
when I stomp on the ground,
and the earth starts to shudder and shake.

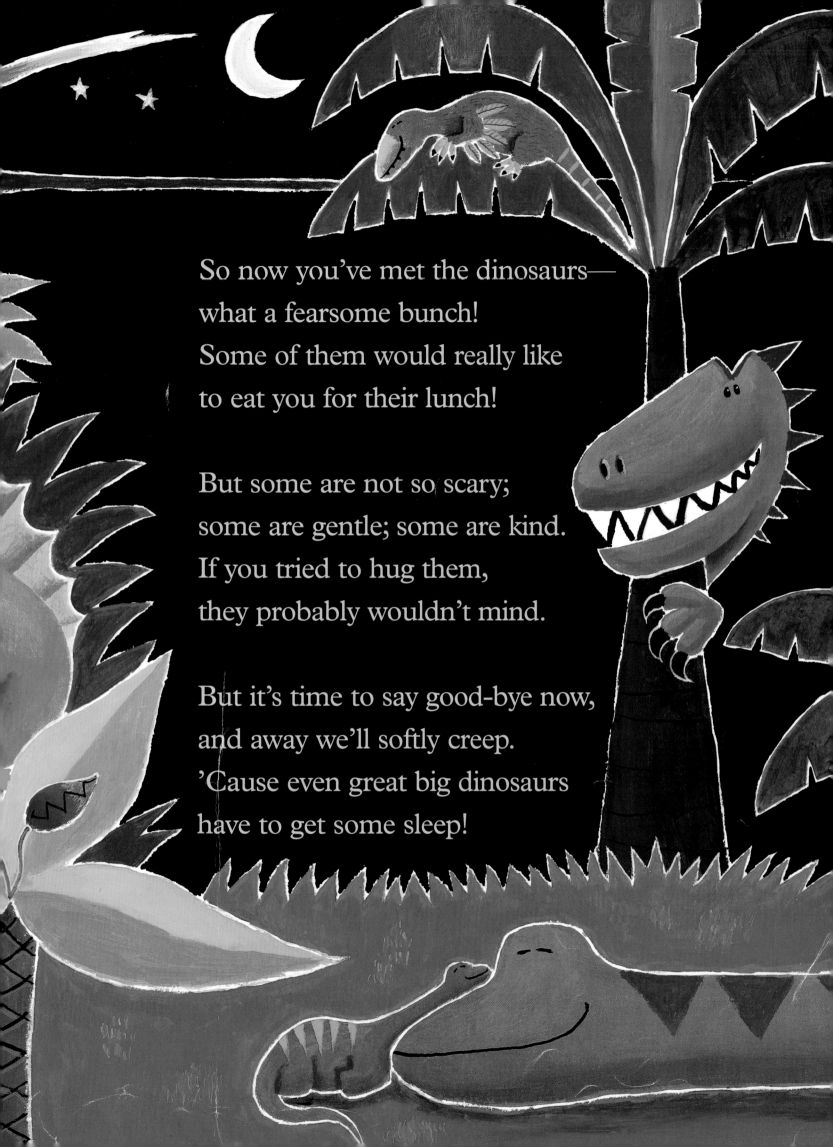

So now you've met the dinosaurs—
what a fearsome bunch!
Some of them would really like
to eat you for their lunch!

But some are not so scary;
some are gentle; some are kind.
If you tried to hug them,
they probably wouldn't mind.

But it's time to say good-bye now,
and away we'll softly creep.
'Cause even great big dinosaurs
have to get some sleep!